THE PUPPY PLACE

SPARKY

THE PUPPY PLACE

Don't miss any of these other stories by Ellen Miles!

THE PUPPY PLACE

SPARKY

ELLEN MILES

SCHOLASTIC INC.

For Jennifer and Choṭi Jyotī, with thanks for the inspiration!

Copyright © 2021 by Ellen Miles
Cover art by Tim O'Brien
Original cover design by Steve Scott

ISBN 978-1-338-68700-2

10 9 8 7 6 5 4 3   21 22 23 24 25

Printed in the U.S.A.   40
First printing 2020

CHAPTER ONE

"All set for your nap, Petey?" Lizzie said as she tucked the soft blanket around her furry friend. She leaned down to kiss him on the nose, and Petey kissed her back, then snuffled happily as he flapped his long ears at her.

Petey was an older Basset hound mix with a gray muzzle, droopy eyes, and silky, floppy ears that hung so low Lizzie sometimes worried he would trip on them. He was one of her favorite dogs at Caring Paws, the animal shelter where she volunteered every Saturday. Petey was so grateful for everything she offered him: a walk outdoors, a biscuit, a soft red fleece blanket she'd made especially for his bed. He'd look up at her with his big, sad hound eyes and wrinkled brow, tilting his head sideways, as if he were saying, "You would do that for little old me?"

Lizzie laughed and bent to give him a hug. Petey loved hugs, and he loved being tucked into his bed for a nap. Lizzie wished someone would come along who would think Petey would make the perfect pet—but so far, nobody had.

"It's hard to find homes for the older dogs," Ms. Dobbins always said. Ms. Dobbins was the director of Caring Paws. "Face it, nothing is as cute as a puppy. And older dogs can be expensive, since many of them need to go to the vet more often."

Lizzie knew Ms. Dobbins spoke from experience. "But if somebody just got to know you, Petey," Lizzie said to Petey now, looking into his big brown eyes. "They'd know you are the sweetest, most patient, most gentle dog in the world. You'd be a perfect dog to have *before* they get a puppy, since a dog like you is the best teacher a puppy can have."

"I know, right?"

Lizzie jumped, surprised by the voice. She hadn't heard any footsteps. But standing right in front of Petey's kennel, with her hand gripping the wire mesh fencing, was a brown-haired girl with a dimply smile and sparkly brown eyes. Lizzie squinted up at her. She thought they looked about the same age, but Lizzie had never seen her at school. "Petey," the girl said nodding. "He's, like, the best dog ever. I can't believe nobody's adopted him."

Who was this girl? And how did she know Petey? Lizzie knew all the regular staff because she spent so much time volunteering. She was curious, but how could she find out more? Would it be rude to just burst out with, "Who are you, anyway?"

Ms. Dobbins walked up just in time. "Oh, great, you two have met," she said. "I know you're going to get along. You have so much in common." She smiled at Lizzie. "Harper has been coming to volunteer three mornings a week for the last month or so," she told her.

Lizzie's eyebrows shot up. That was a lot of volunteering. How did she have so much time, this Harper person?

"I'm homeschooled," Harper said, as if to answer the question Lizzie had not asked out loud. "I get most of my schoolwork done really early in the morning. Then my mom and I come here, and afterward we go back home and I finish up the rest of my lessons."

"She's been a big help," said Ms. Dobbins. "Harper knows so much about dogs and how to care for them."

Lizzie tried to look happy about that, but she couldn't help but feel a twinge of envy. She was the one who knew the most about dogs. She was the one who Ms. Dobbins called her "superstar volunteer." She was the responsible one, the only volunteer under fourteen who was allowed to walk the shelter dogs on her own. Lizzie took a breath. "Cool," she said.

Ms. Dobbins laughed. "Oh, but of course Harper still has plenty to learn," she said. She turned to Harper. "Lizzie is one of our longest-term volunteers. She's taught *me* things I didn't know about dogs. Plus, she's great with all the animals and very responsible. Her family fosters puppies, so I know I can trust her with just about any dog."

Lizzie felt better for a second. Until Harper said, "Oh, so she's the other girl who's allowed to walk the dogs?"

Lizzie blinked, squeezed her eyes shut, then opened them again wide. "Wait, what?" she asked.

Ms. Dobbins smiled and nodded. "That's right," she said. "Harper has proved herself to me, just like you did, Lizzie. Now she's a dog walker, too. I think you'll be glad for the help. Harper's also going to start coming in on Saturdays, just like you."

Lizzie smiled, but it was only with her mouth. She wasn't really all that excited to hear that this Harper person was going to be there at the same time she was. Three mornings a week—wasn't that enough? Now she had to horn in on Lizzie's time, too?

"I heard there are some different routines on Saturdays," Harper said. "Maybe you can help me learn?" She smiled at Lizzie. Her smile wasn't fake, like Lizzie's had been. Lizzie could tell by the way Harper's eyes crinkled up and her dimples deepened.

"Sure," said Lizzie, shrugging. What else could she say? She gave Petey one more pat and wiped her hands on the towel hanging by his door. "Saturday's a day when we can get a lot of visitors, so we like to make sure everything—including the dogs—looks good. That means we do a lot of cleaning." Lizzie glanced at Ms. Dobbins, who nodded approvingly, then winked at Lizzie and headed off toward her office. Lizzie was hoping that Harper would be scared off by the idea of cleaning, but she followed Lizzie down the hall, chatting.

"I'm a pretty good sweeper," said Harper. "That's one of my chores at home. And I actually love mopping, too, believe it or not."

Lizzie led Harper to the utility closet and showed her where all the cleaning supplies were kept. "I usually start with brushing the dogs," Lizzie said. "That way they're all shiny and ready to meet the public. Then we do the sweeping and mopping afterward, so we clean up all the hair they shed."

"I'm used to that," said Harper. "We have two Samoyeds."

Lizzie couldn't help laughing. She knew that the fluffy white dogs were legendary shedders. She handed Harper a brush and took one for herself. "You can start at this end, with Elmo, and I'll start at the other."

"Aw, I love Elmo!" said Harper.

That made Lizzie like Harper a little more. Elmo, a terrier-Chihuahua mix, wasn't the cutest or the smartest little dog. He had a funny long tooth that stuck out and his fur was scruffy and he smelled not so great, but he had such a likable personality. "I know. There's just something about him," Lizzie said.

She walked Harper to Elmo's kennel, and they laughed when they saw that he was already standing with his front paws against the door. His tiny, scruffy tail was wagging hard. "He must have heard us talking about him," said Lizzie, bending down to scratch him through the wire cage.

"So your family fosters puppies? I'm so jelly," said Harper.

Lizzie nodded. Good. She sort of liked that Harper was jealous. "We've fostered so many! My younger brother, Charles, helps a lot, and my youngest brother, the Bean, likes to play with them. We even got to keep one, the best puppy ever. His name's Buddy, and we ended up adopting him."

Then Lizzie straightened up, clearing her throat. "Anyway, it looks like Elmo could really use a brushing. I guess that's not something you ever get around to when you come in on weekdays."

Harper blinked. "Well," she began, but just then, through the kennel's open windows, Lizzie heard a car zoom into the parking lot and skid to a stop. Two car doors slammed, one right after the other. Footsteps pounded up the outside stairs, and the door to the reception area flew open.

Lizzie looked at Harper, her heart beating fast. "Something's going on," she said. "An emergency."

They threw down their brushes and ran for the door.

CHAPTER TWO

"What's going on?" asked Lizzie as she and Harper burst through the door into the reception area. The small room, usually peaceful, was full of movement and noise. "Hold on, Lizzie." Ms. Dobbins held up a hand. "We've got a situation here."

Something in Ms. Dobbins's tone made Lizzie freeze in place. The shelter director turned back to a scruffy man and a woman huddled near the front desk, holding something wrapped in a dark green blanket. "When did you find him?" she asked. "Where?" She reached out her arms.

Harper, who had frozen mid-step next to Lizzie, stood on her tiptoes to try to get a look over Ms.

Dobbins's shoulder. Lizzie took a few quiet steps forward. She craned her neck. What was wrapped in the blanket?

"It's a puppy," said the bearded man. His hair was mussed and he had a smudge of dirt on his cheek. "Just a little guy." He choked up and stopped talking.

The woman put her arm around him. "Derek, it's okay. They're going to help him here."

"I hope we can," said Ms. Dobbins. "What kind of help does he need?" Now she was holding the blanket. Lizzie tiptoed three steps closer, but she still couldn't see.

"His leg, it's his leg," said the woman. "Something's just not right with it." Tears were running down her cheeks. "And he's so skinny and weak. He can hardly move."

"We think he must have been abandoned!" said the man. "Maybe because of his leg. We were out for a walk, and we heard this whimpering sound, and we went to look under a bush, and there he was, just lying there all alone. He can barely move."

Ms. Dobbins was nodding. "But he let you pick him up?" she asked.

"That's the funny thing," said the woman. "He made his way over to me as soon I knelt down and called to him. And he settled in my lap on the way over here. He's a total cuddlebug." She sniffed and tears started to roll down her face again. "How could he ever trust humans after somebody left him like that?"

"You did the right thing," said Ms. Dobbins softly, patting the woman's shoulder. Then she peeled back the blanket to take a look. Lizzie saw a pointy little nose. She saw two bright, inquisitive eyes. And she saw two triangular ears, standing straight at attention as the puppy stared straight back at her. The puppy did not look nearly as upset as the people did. He looked curious. His ears swiveled around and his nose twitched as he tried to figure out his new surroundings.

Whoa, what just happened? One minute I was in my special hidey-hole, and the next minute—here I am! I mean, where am I?

"If he's badly injured, we can't help him here," said Ms. Dobbins. "We don't have a vet on our staff." She was still peeling the blanket away. "But one way or another, he's going to have to see a vet. He's starved and probably dehydrated. Lizzie, call Dr. Gibson's office," Ms. Dobbins said. "Tell them we're coming right over with an injured puppy."

Lizzie didn't move. She couldn't. She felt frozen in place, stuck in her spot, unable to think about what to do next. She'd always wondered how well she would do in an emergency, and now she was finding out.

"Um, Lizzie, I can take care of the call. But we're going to need some more blankets," said Harper, giving Lizzie a little push toward the storeroom. "You know where they are, right?"

Lizzie nodded. She did know. She didn't like being bossed around by Harper, but it seemed like more blankets would be a good idea. Not that she even knew what was happening, but from the look on Ms. Dobbins's face, it was serious.

As she turned to go, she saw Harper slip behind the counter and pick up the telephone receiver. Harper leaned down to look at the phone list taped to the counter, then dialed quickly. By the time Lizzie came back out of the storeroom with a pile of folded blankets in her arms, Harper was talking to someone at Dr. Gibson's office. "Yes, we're at Caring Paws," she said. "Yes, we're coming right over."

Lizzie was still annoyed with herself for freezing like that, but she couldn't help feeling impressed by Harper's cool head. Apparently she was very good in an emergency, or at least in this one.

The woman reached out to put a hand on Ms. Dobbins's arm. "You'll help him?" she asked.

"We'll do our best," said Ms. Dobbins.

Lizzie approached her, holding out one of the blankets from the storeroom. "Good," said Ms. Dobbins. "We'll make him extra cozy so he doesn't get cold. He seems okay so far, but that could change if he goes into shock. Keeping him warm will help prevent that." She nodded at Lizzie, and Lizzie did her best to tuck her blanket around the dark green one already swaddling the pup.

"We'll get your blanket back to you as soon as we can," Ms. Dobbins told the couple.

"No need!" the man said, holding up his hands. "It's just an old army blanket I had in the trunk. It's full of holes. Just—take care of the puppy, okay?"

He peered down at the tiny pup. "Hang in there, little dude," he said.

"Lizzie, take those other blankets out to my car and make a nice bed for him, on the backseat." Ms. Dobbins gestured toward the front door with her chin. "You and Harper come with me. You can sit on either side of him so he doesn't budge. Once we're on our way, you can call your parents and let them know you're with me."

She turned to nod at the couple. "You did the right thing to bring him in," she said. "Thanks for caring about animals."

The woman nodded and sniffed, wiping her

eyes. "Can we call to find out what happened?" she asked. The man put his arm around her and held her close.

"Of course you can," said Ms. Dobbins. "I hope you will."

Lizzie and Harper ran out to the parking lot, to Ms. Dobbins's small red car. Harper opened one back door and Lizzie opened the other. Then they arranged the blankets into a cozy nest for the puppy.

Their eyes met across the seat. "I hope he's going to be okay," Lizzie whispered.

"I hope so, too," Harper whispered back.

CHAPTER THREE

Lizzie knew that it was only a few miles between the animal shelter and Dr. Gibson's office, but the drive seemed to take forever. While she used Ms. Dobbins's phone to call her mom, she kept one hand on top of the blanket covering the puppy. She could feel him shivering. "He's so young to be on his own," she said when she'd finished her call and passed the phone to Harper.

Harper nodded. "I'm wondering if his mom was also a stray," she said.

"I have a feeling she was," said Ms. Dobbins from the front seat. "This puppy looks like he's been living rough."

Lizzie felt like saying that she'd had the same thought, but did it really matter right now? "I wonder if he's been weaned," she said instead. "If he was part of a stray litter maybe he and his siblings were still living on their mom's milk."

"Good point," said Ms. Dobbins. "He'll need to be bottle-fed if that's the case."

"I've never done that," said Harper. "But I'd like to learn how."

"We did it with a puppy that my family fostered. Bella," said Lizzie, remembering the tiny cocker spaniel puppy. "It's a lot of work."

"I'd like to help," said Harper.

"It'll all depend on what Dr. Gibson says after she's examined the patient," said Ms. Dobbins. "Let's just wait and see what she thinks."

Lizzie sat back, still holding her hand steady against the puppy's tiny, shivering body. "We'll take care of you, no matter what," she whispered.

She didn't care if Harper thought she was weird for talking to a puppy.

"Definitely," Harper told the puppy. "We promise."

Lizzie gave her a small smile.

Ms. Dobbins pulled up in front of the vet's office a few minutes later. "Stay put, you two," she said as she got out of the car. She came around to Lizzie's side and opened the door. "Okay, now hand him to me, gently."

Lizzie scooped up the mound of blankets, making sure to support the puppy wrapped inside. He hardly weighed a thing. She handed the bundle to Ms. Dobbins, then unbuckled her seat belt, got out, and ran to open the door to the vet's office.

"That was quick," said Dr. Gibson, meeting them at the reception desk. She peeled off a pair of light blue rubber gloves. "Perfect timing. I just finished with another patient. Come on back and we'll see what we've got here." She led the way to the exam room. Ms. Dobbins took a seat, the blanket bundle on her lap, and Lizzie and Harper stood on either side of her.

Dr. Gibson went to the sink and washed her hands. "So, tell me what you've brought me," she said over her shoulder.

"It's a very young pup with an injured leg," said Ms. Dobbins. "He might be in shock, since he probably hasn't eaten or drunk anything for a while."

Dr. Gibson put on a new pair of gloves and then took the blanket bundle from Ms. Dobbins. Slowly and carefully, she set it on her high, stainless-steel exam table, and unwrapped it all the way.

"Ohhhh," Lizzie and Harper both said at the same time.

The puppy was adorable, brown with white markings. Lizzie thought he looked like some kind of Chihuahua mix, with his delicate, tiny feet and big brown eyes. He held his little tail between his legs as he stood shivering. He stared up at Dr. Gibson with bright eyes and cocked his head sideways. His triangular ears stood at attention.

Another new place! I should be scared, but somehow I'm not. I think these people want to help me.

Dr. Gibson smiled down at him. "Hey, there," she said. "I don't know your name, but I'm going to call you Sparky, 'cause I can tell you're one tough and feisty little dude. You've been through some hard times, haven't you?" She touched him gently all over, starting at his shoulders, then his head, his front legs, then carefully along his ribs and spine. Finally, she touched his back legs. Lizzie watched closely and saw how the pup flinched a bit when she touched his back right leg.

"That's where he hurts," Lizzie said.

Dr. Gibson nodded. "Yes, it is." She continued to touch the puppy very gently, moving the leg carefully. "It's hard to say what's wrong," she said. "There's no blood or scar, so it's possible he was even born this way. Either way, he's probably been living with this injury for a while. He's small, but he's not as young as you'd think. He's undernourished." She laid both hands on the puppy. "We're done, sweetie. Let's get you cozied back up in your blankets and hooked up to some fluids." She pressed an intercom button and asked her vet tech to come in to help start an IV.

"We'll shave his front leg just a little, then put a needle there so we can give him some fluids through a line," Dr. Gibson explained. "It's the best way to help him feel better in a hurry. He can rest while that's happening, and we can figure out our next steps."

"Won't that hurt him?" Lizzie's heart ached for the little guy. She was dying to cuddle and pet him, but she knew she would have to wait.

"Only a tiny bit for a moment," said Dr. Gibson. "Gloria is very good at this." She smiled at the young woman who had come into the room, wheeling a stand that held a bag of clear liquid with a long plastic line coming out of it.

"I want to be a vet when I grow up," said Harper. She stepped closer for a better view.

Lizzie had often thought about being a vet, too. But she discovered that she didn't really want a closer look. She watched as Gloria used an electric clipper to shave the puppy's leg. But she had to look away when the tech picked up the needle. It was just like back at Caring Paws, the way Harper stepped up when Lizzie froze. Why was she acting so hesitant?

Ms. Dobbins put her arm around Lizzie. "It's

hard to watch," she said, squeezing Lizzie's shoulder. "But it really will make him feel better."

"What about his hurt leg?" Lizzie asked Dr. Gibson. "Can you fix it?"

The vet shook her head as she pulled off her gloves. "I don't think so, Lizzie."

Lizzie's heart fell. The poor little puppy.

CHAPTER FOUR

"But I know someone who might be able to," Dr. Gibson went on. "My friend Josephine is one of the best animal surgeons in the area. I'll give her a call."

"A surgeon?" Lizzie asked. "You mean—Sparky might have to have an operation?"

Dr. Gibson nodded. "Yes. It would be worth it if Dr. Jo can make Sparky's leg work right again."

"And if not?" Ms. Dobbins asked.

Dr. Gibson raised her eyebrows. "Let's cross that bridge when we come to it," she said.

Lizzie had the feeling that there was something the vet did not want to discuss in front of her and Harper. She wanted to tell Dr. Gibson that they could take it, that she could say anything in front of them, but there was also a part of her that didn't want to hear it. Whatever it was, it was super serious. Lizzie could see that, plain as anything, on Dr. Gibson's face.

"I'm guessing Dr. Jo won't be able to see him until tomorrow, so we'll keep the puppy here tonight," said Dr. Gibson. "I want to keep giving him fluids and also try to feed him something. He's so skinny! We have to beef him up so he looks more like a nice pudgy puppy." As she spoke, she cradled the puppy in her arms. "Isn't that right, Sparky?" she asked in a funny squeaky voice.

The puppy cocked his head and blinked, then let his mouth fall open in a wide doggy grin. Lizzie even saw that he was doing his best to wag his tail, but he seemed too weak to really make it move.

You bet! I'm totally up for whatever.

Lizzie's eyes filled with tears. This puppy was so spunky! "I think you picked the perfect name for him," she said to Dr. Gibson. She knew that the vet was trying to lighten things up, which was a good idea. Sparky needed all the good energy they could send his way.

"Will—will he be a little stronger by tomorrow?" asked Harper.

Lizzie could see that Harper was upset. She was frowning and biting her lip. Lizzie noticed that Harper's fingers were crossed, wishing the best for Sparky. Lizzie got it. She felt the same, and had both her fingers and her toes crossed.

"Definitely. I guarantee it," said Dr. Gibson. "He just needs some food, some water, and some rest." She walked closer to Lizzie and Harper, carrying

Sparky. "Want to give him a little pet before I get him settled for the night?"

Lizzie stroked his tiny head with one finger. "Night-night, Sparky," she whispered.

Harper touched his front paw. "Sleep tight," she said.

Then Ms. Dobbins knelt down and stroked the puppy all over, very gently and slowly. Lizzie saw Sparky's eyelids close, then blink open again. He definitely needed some sleep. When Ms. Dobbins stood up, she wiped the tears out of her eyes. "We'll see you first thing tomorrow, you little peanut," she said.

Lizzie had heard Ms. Dobbins talk to a lot of dogs. She did it all the time, in the kennels or the exercise yard at the shelter. But she'd never heard her talk like this, so softly and lovingly. She put her hand on Ms. Dobbins's arm. "He'll be okay," Lizzie said.

Ms. Dobbins pulled out a tissue and blew her nose. "I know," she said, nodding to Lizzie—and to Harper, who was patting her other arm. "Okay, girls. Let's get you home. It's time to say good night to Sparky."

"Good night, pal," said Harper.

"See you tomorrow, Sparky," said Lizzie.

"We know he couldn't be in better hands," Ms. Dobbins said to Dr. Gibson. "Thanks so mu-mu-much." She was starting to cry again. Lizzie and Harper guided her out the door. They stood outside for a moment, until they all stopped crying. Then Ms. Dobbins led them to the car. She shook her head as she pulled out of the parking lot a few moments later. "This is one of the reasons why I don't have a dog of my own," she said. "There are times when it's just too—too—"

"Sad?" Harper asked.

"Scary?" Lizzie suggested.

"Heartbreaking," said Ms. Dobbins. Lizzie saw her bite her lip to keep from crying. Then Ms. Dobbins took a deep breath and put on a smile. "But Dr. Gibson has a lot of experience, and I bet she's right. I'm sure Sparky will look and feel a ton better tomorrow."

"Me, too," said Harper.

"Me, three," said Lizzie. She knew they were all pretending a little bit, but so what? It was good to be optimistic. "You know," she added, "I've helped take care of a lot of sick puppies and injured puppies, and I've never seen one that had as much spirit as Sparky."

Ms. Dobbins nodded thoughtfully. "You're right," she said slowly. "He really is a fighter, in the best sense. He'll be just fine."

"Yeah, Sparky! Go, Sparky!" Harper punched her fist in the air like she was rooting for her favorite team.

Ms. Dobbins pulled the car up in front of Lizzie's house. "First stop," she said. "Tell your mom I'm sorry you're late for dinner."

Lizzie unbuckled, said good-bye to Harper, and got out of the car, then leaned back in for a moment before she shut the door. "And you'll pick me up first thing tomorrow when you go to see Sparky?" she asked.

Ms. Dobbins nodded and smiled. "Of course," she said. "Try not to worry. Remember, Dr. Gibson says Dr. Jo is the best. We're in good hands."

CHAPTER FIVE

Lizzie dropped her backpack in the front hall and ran straight into her mother's arms. "Aw, honey," her mom said, stroking her back. "Hard day at the shelter, huh?"

"He—he's so little and so cute." Lizzie was sobbing. She had held it together until now, but suddenly she couldn't keep her tears back anymore.

"Come, tell me all about it." Her mom took Lizzie's hand and brought her into the living room. Lizzie sat on her mother's lap—something she hardly ever did these days—and told her the whole story.

"Sparky sounds like an amazing pup," said Mrs. Peterson, when Lizzie finished. "I bet he's going to be just fine." Mom hugged Lizzie tight. "Now, how about some dinner? The rest of us already ate, but I saved plenty for you. Charles and Dad are in the den playing Uno, and the Bean is in bed."

Lizzie realized she was starving. She sat down at the kitchen table and gulped down mashed potatoes and meat loaf as if she'd never seen food before. "I hope Sparky's getting some food, too," she said when she stopped long enough to talk.

Mom smiled. "Probably not meat loaf, but I'm sure they're getting some nutrition into him. Now, how about if we run you a nice hot bath? Then you can get into your p.j.'s and maybe you and I can watch a movie together."

The bath happened, and the p.j.'s, but by then Lizzie couldn't keep her eyes open. "We'll watch the movie tomorrow," her mom said as she tucked her in.

"Tomorrow," Lizzie mumbled, her eyes already closing. "And maybe Sparky's leg will be fixed by then, too."

When Lizzie first woke up, everything seemed normal. Buddy was curled in a soft, warm circle near her feet. Her blankets felt cozy. Sun streamed through her bedroom window, leaf-shaped shadows dappling the curtains. Lizzie yawned. She stretched. She sat up and gave Buddy a scritch right where he liked it, between his shoulder blades.

Then she remembered.

Sparky. She felt a pang of sadness, thinking of his adorable little foxy face and big shiny eyes as she had said good-bye the day before. Then she remembered the puppy's upright ears and his attempts to wag his tail. She remembered his happy spirit, and she felt a surge of hope.

Lizzie pulled on jeans and a T-shirt, brushed her teeth for ten seconds, and ran down the stairs, with Buddy at her heels. "Mom," she said as she burst into the kitchen. "I've been thinking!"

"So have I," said her mom, hands on her hips. "I've been thinking that you need a good, solid breakfast this morning because it could be a long day." She pointed to the kitchen table. "Sit," she said. "I made waffles."

Mom knew that Lizzie couldn't resist waffles. "But Ms. Dobbins might be here any minute. And Buddy needs to go out."

Mom nodded. "I know. I'll take him out back. But you sit here and eat."

Lizzie wanted to protest, but suddenly the unmistakable smell of waffles, doused in butter and maple syrup, wafted up into her nose. She looked down at the plate in front of her, picked up her fork, and dug in.

When Mom and Buddy came back in, Lizzie took her chance. "Mom, I wanted to ask you. If the puppy is allowed to go home after his surgery— well, he doesn't have a home, really. So, we can foster him, right?"

"Oh, Lizzie," said Mom. "That's a big responsibility. We'll have to talk to your dad about that idea."

"Okay." Lizzie nodded, smiling to herself. If her brother Charles hadn't still been sleeping like a lazybones, he would have smiled back at her. They both knew that Dad always said yes to new foster pups. And Mom could never turn down someone in need. So, basically, it was a yes. Maybe she would be able to bring Sparky home that very day!

Lizzie dug happily back into her waffles. She was swallowing the last bite when she heard a car horn honk outside. "She's here!" she said to her mom, pushing back from the table. "I have to go!" She grabbed her backpack and a jacket and headed for the front door. Then she stopped in her tracks, turned around, and dashed back into the kitchen to throw her arms around her mom. "Thanks for the waffles," she said. In her mind, she added, *And thanks for saying that we can foster Sparky!*

She ran out the door and down the front walk and up to Ms. Dobbins's car. She grabbed at the handle of the front passenger-side door before she realized that someone was already in that seat. Harper.

CHAPTER SIX

"Good morning!" sang out Harper, as Lizzie climbed into the backseat.

"Good morning," Lizzie answered, a little less enthusiastically. Why did Harper have to come along again today? Lizzie had been picturing just herself and Ms. Dobbins taking Sparky to see the surgeon.

Ms. Dobbins nodded from the front seat. "Morning, Lizzie."

She looked tired, and her clothes—the same blouse and pants she'd been wearing the day before—were wrinkled. She met Lizzie's eyes in the rearview mirror. "I know, I'm not looking my best," she said. "I went back and spent the night on a couch at Dr. Gibson's, near the kennels. Didn't want that poor little pup to wake up with nobody there."

Lizzie was surprised. She'd never heard of Ms. Dobbins doing something like that before. "That's good," she said. "So how is he? How's Sparky?"

Ms. Dobbins smiled. "He really is better, just like Dr. Gibson promised. You'll see. But still, the little guy needs all the help he can get." She met Lizzie's eyes in the rearview mirror, and Lizzie got the message. If Harper wanted to help, that was a good thing.

"I brought him a toy," said Harper, holding up a stuffed goose.

"Cute," said Lizzie, wishing she had thought of that.

When they pulled up outside the vet's office, Dr. Gibson was waiting for them. With Sparky! On a leash!

Lizzie snatched off her seat belt and pushed out of the car as soon as it stopped. "Wow," she said. Sparky really did seem so much better than he had the day before. His eyes twinkled as he looked back at her. He limped down the front walkway, dragging his hurt leg along. Lizzie was surprised at how fast he could move. It seemed like his hurt leg wasn't slowing him down that much.

Hi, friend! I remember you from yesterday, even though I was pretty out of it. Want to play?

"Incredible difference, isn't it?" Dr. Gibson asked Lizzie. "I think he may have been limping that way all his life, but he manages pretty well.

He basically just needed some water and some nutrition, and now he's raring to go."

"But we're still taking him to the surgeon, right?" Lizzie asked, stooping down to give Sparky a pat. "He can't limp around like this forever."

"Absolutely, we're taking him. In fact, he's ready to go and so am I. Shall we?" She gestured back at the car. Ms. Dobbins and Harper hadn't even gotten out yet.

Harper got into the backseat so Dr. Gibson could sit up front. As he had the day before, Sparky lay between the two girls on a nest of blankets. But unlike the day before, he was perky—paying attention to everything that happened inside and outside the car. When Lizzie petted him, he leaned over to put a paw on her leg and stretched up his neck to give her a kiss on the cheek. When

Harper showed him the stuffed goose, he grabbed it in his teeth and gave it a little shake. Then he sat up on his blankets, ears and nose twitching, watching the scenery go by.

Wow, it's a big world out here. Who knew?

Lizzie couldn't stop smiling. Sparky was going to be okay after all. She could tell. And as long as Dad said yes—which she was sure he would—the chances were good that she and her family would be fostering him very soon.

Ms. Dobbins pulled up in front of a low, modern building. "This is it, right?" she asked Dr. Gibson.

"This is it," said the vet. "And there's Dr. Jo, waiting for us." She waved at a woman dressed in green scrubs who stood in the doorway of the clinic. The woman waved back and came out to meet them.

"So this is our patient," said the dark-haired woman. "What a cutie!"

Lizzie climbed out of the car with Sparky in her arms.

Dr. Jo reached out and Lizzie handed Sparky over. After the surgeon nuzzled him a bit and whispered some baby talk into his ear, she introduced herself, and they all told her their names. Then they followed her inside.

"I'll do a quick exam while you're here," said Dr. Jo as she led them into a high-tech examining room with all sorts of fancy machines against the walls. "But we'll need to keep him overnight in order to run some more tests and make a plan."

Lizzie's face fell. She realized now that she had been too optimistic to think she might be able to take Sparky home with her that night. But the most important thing was for him to get his leg fixed.

Dr. Jo set Sparky on her exam table, petting the tiny puppy gently to calm him. She used her stethoscope to listen to his heart and lungs, then looked into his ears and mouth, moving slowly and carefully. Finally, she touched him all over. He flinched, just as he had the day before, when she touched his back right leg. "Mm-hmm," said Dr. Jo. She felt the leg all over, moving it this way and that, sometimes with her eyes closed. "Mm-hmm" she said again, when she stepped back. She pulled off her gloves, deep in thought.

Ms. Dobbins was biting her lip.

Harper was looking down at her feet.

Lizzie couldn't take the silence anymore. "So what do you think?" she asked. "Can you make Sparky's leg better?"

"We'll see," said Dr. Jo. "I promise I'll do my best, if the X-rays and MRI show that the leg can be saved." Then her face grew serious. "That's kind of a big *if*," she added, "from what I can tell from my physical exam."

Nobody talked during the ride home. Ms. Dobbins's car was silent as they thought about poor little Sparky. He'd been so cute when they said good-bye, blinking up at all of them with his twinkly eyes. It was like he was letting them know that everything would be okay.

Lizzie wanted to ask more about what would happen if Dr. Jo couldn't fix Sparky's leg, but she had a feeling she did not want to hear the answer, so she kept quiet. She decided to just wait and see what the surgeon had to say the next day. In the meantime, she'd be hoping for the best.

CHAPTER SEVEN

Lizzie, Harper, and Ms. Dobbins headed back to the surgeon's office the next afternoon, eager to see Sparky and hear what Dr. Jo had to tell them. The surgeon had phoned Ms. Dobbins to say she had news, and Ms. Dobbins had picked Lizzie up right after school. Of course, Harper was in the car, too. Lizzie still wasn't used to her being around all the time. Was Harper Ms. Dobbins's new favorite? Lizzie tried not to worry about that. There were bigger things to worry about, like how Sparky was doing.

"Hi, I'm Layla, Dr. Jo's assistant." A young woman in yellow scrubs met them at the door and stuck a hand out for Lizzie to shake. Then she shook with Harper and Ms. Dobbins, too.

Lizzie craned her neck to peek down the hall past Layla. Where was Sparky? She couldn't wait to see him. This time she'd brought him a toy, a type of bouncy, chewy ball that Buddy loved. She knew Sparky would like it, too.

"Dr. Jo asked me to have you wait in her office," said Layla. She began to move to a door at the right of the reception desk. Lizzie saw that Harper was looking down the hallway, too. "Um, this way, girls." Layla smiled at them. "You'll see Sparky soon, I promise."

"Can he go home today?" Lizzie asked. "I mean, he doesn't actually have a home, but you know what I mean."

"I'll let Dr. Jo answer that," said Layla.

Lizzie exchanged a worried look with Harper.

"Please, don't worry." Layla must have noticed.

She flashed them another smile. "Dr. Jo will explain everything. And it's really lucky you brought Sparky here. Dr. Jo is the best."

Lizzie and Harper let themselves be led to Dr. Jo's office, along with Ms. Dobbins. The space was tiny. It was crammed with file cabinets, a desk covered in papers, two bookcases full of thick books, dog food samples, piles of magazines, and—"Hey, look at those cats!" said Lizzie, pointing to the top of one of the bookshelves. "How did they even get all the way up there?" One cat was gray, with green eyes. The other was black, with a little spot of white on his chest. They looked down with interest at the people who had come into their space.

Layla laughed. "Meet Yogi and Moxie," she said. "They're kind of our office mascots. Yogi is the gray one." She made a kissy noise, and the cats looked down at her, tails twitching. Then

Yogi stood up, stretched, and picked his way delicately down from the bookshelf. Moxie took one big leap and landed with a thump in the middle of the desk. Layla scratched each cat under his chin as she reached into the pocket of her scrubs for a treat.

"Please, have a seat," she said, waving a hand around. "I mean, if you can find somewhere. Dr. Jo is really too busy to ever use this office, so it ends up a little messy."

Ms. Dobbins perched on a file cabinet. Lizzie leaned on the desk. Harper picked up a pile of books to reveal a stool to sit on. Lizzie reached over to pet Yogi. He pushed his head against her hand, a rumbly purr rising from his throat. Then he nudged at her again until she scooped him onto her lap. "Aw," she said. "You're a lovebug, just like Sparky."

Lizzie was still holding Yogi when Dr. Jo came

into the office, wearing a white coat over her scrubs. "Ah, you've met our caretakers, I see," she said. "I always say this place just wouldn't function right without Yogi and Moxie on board."

"They're sweet," said Lizzie. The weight of the cat in her arms was comforting somehow. But it didn't distract her from the main thing on her mind. "What about Sparky? How is he? Can I take him home tonight?"

Lizzie saw Harper's eyebrows go up, as if she was surprised to hear that Lizzie planned to foster Sparky as he healed. But Lizzie plowed ahead. "My mom and dad talked about it last night and agreed that we can foster Sparky. We know he'll need extra care, but we're ready."

Dr. Jo sat down in the desk chair and tented her hands beneath her chin. "Okay, look. I'm not going to make you wait any longer. Here's the deal with Sparky."

Lizzie held her breath.

"There's good news and not-so-good news," said Dr. Jo. "The good news is that we went ahead and did surgery on Sparky last night, and he came through it beautifully. He's doing great, and yes— he will be able to leave our clinic tonight."

Lizzie grinned. That wasn't just good news, it was great news.

"But here's the not-so-good news," said Dr. Jo. "We tried to fix his leg, but . . . well, we couldn't. We realized almost right away that it was damaged beyond repair."

"Mm-hmm," said Ms. Dobbins, who was nodding as if she'd expected this. "So you had to—"

Dr. Jo nodded. She looked first at Lizzie, then at Harper. "Do you girls know what amputation means?" she asked.

Harper nodded, so Lizzie did, too. But she didn't really know, not exactly.

"It's when something gets cut off, right?" asked Harper.

"Exactly," said Dr. Jo. "When we couldn't save Sparky's leg, that's what we had to do."

Lizzie couldn't believe it. Her stomach was in knots. This was terrible. "What? So Sparky only has three legs now?" she asked.

Dr. Jo nodded. "I know, it sounds bad. But do some research. You'll see. Three-legged dogs can have fantastic lives, just like any other dog."

"Sparky is a tripawd now!" said Ms. Dobbins.

Dr. Jo smiled. "Yup. And I think he's going to be just fine with that. Better than dragging that hurt leg around for the rest of his life."

"I think I saw a video about tripawds," said Harper.

Dr. Jo stood up. "Look," she said, gazing right at Lizzie. "I know this is a lot to take in, but let's go see Sparky and say hi. Then you can go home and learn about tripawds. I think you'll be very surprised."

Back in the kennel area of the clinic, Sparky lay quietly on a soft, green bed in a clean kennel. He wore a plastic collar around his neck, a big cone that encircled his head. "That's to keep him from licking or biting at himself as he heals," said Dr. Jo.

That was when Lizzie let her eyes go to Sparky's back right leg. The leg that—wasn't there! A big white bandage was in its place, over his hip. She felt tears spring to her eyes. "Sparky," she whispered. She saw his eyes flicker and caught the tiny motion of his tail as he tried to wag it.

"He's pretty out of it right now," said Dr. Jo, putting a hand on Lizzie's back. "He'll be a bit livelier later on, but when you get him home this evening he'll still probably just want to sleep."

Lizzie gulped. She'd been all set to foster

Sparky—but that was before he was a tripawd. Suddenly, she felt a lot less sure. In fact, she felt that same feeling she'd felt when he was first brought into Caring Paws. Overwhelmed. Frozen in place. Was a three-legged dog more than she was ready to handle?

CHAPTER EIGHT

"Where's the puppy?" Charles asked when Lizzie got home. "Mom told me we might have a new foster puppy."

The knot in Lizzie's stomach had only gotten bigger on the way home. She shook her head. "Not—not yet," she told her brother. "He had kind of a big operation. He can leave the vet's office tonight, but—" Lizzie clammed up. She didn't want to confess that she was overwhelmed by the responsibility of taking care of a three-legged puppy. For that matter, she didn't want to have to explain about amputation to her younger brother.

He'd probably be even more upset by the idea than she was.

But Charles still had questions. "Did they fix his leg?" he asked.

Lizzie rolled her eyes. Mom must have told him everything. "No," she said softly. "They couldn't. They had to, um—"

"Amputate?" Charles asked. "I know all about that. My friend's cousin has a three-legged dog and he does great. You should see him run all over their yard! He's faster than most four-legged dogs."

Lizzie wished she could feel that optimistic. But she couldn't shake the image of poor little Sparky, curled into a tiny ball with that cone over his head. And the big bandage on his hip . . . "Where's Mom?" Lizzie asked. She needed a hug.

"She took the Bean to the playground," said Charles. "And Dad's in the garage."

A Dad hug was just as good as a Mom hug. Lizzie went to find him.

"Hey, sweetie," he said, looking up from a pile of junk he was sorting. "Awww," he added, as soon as he saw her face. He stood up and opened his arms. "Come here, sugar pie."

She ran to him and he held her tightly as she cried into his shoulder. "He's so little," she sobbed. "And so sweet."

"But he's okay?" Dad asked. "Did they save Sparky's leg?"

Lizzie stood back and shook her head. Then she started to sob again as she explained what had happened.

"That's really tough. But I hear that three-legged dogs can have great lives," Dad said.

Lizzie wailed louder. "That's what everybody says." She pulled away. "I'm going to my room," she said. She needed to be alone for a while. She didn't even want to see Buddy right then, with his four strong, healthy legs.

Dad gave her one more squeeze, then let her go. "Okay, but I'm going to come see you soon," he said.

Lizzie ran upstairs and into her room, slamming the door behind her. She threw herself down on the bed and cried for a while longer, until she couldn't cry anymore. Then she lay on her back, wondering why everybody seemed to think it was no big deal that this adorable, tiny puppy had lost a leg.

There was a tap at her door. "Come in," Lizzie said, expecting her dad.

It wasn't Dad. It was Mom, back from the playground. "Tough day?" she asked, plopping herself down on the bed.

Lizzie felt like crying again, but she didn't seem to have any tears left. "Hi," she said.

"Dad told me about Sparky," said Mom. "I figured you could use some company." She lay down next to Lizzie. "It's awful," she said. "I can't stand to see any dog hurting."

Lizzie sniffled. "And everybody acts like it's no big deal," she said.

Mom nodded. "They're wrong. It's a big deal," she said. Then she turned onto her side and looked into Lizzie's eyes. "But here's the thing: He will heal, and he will be fine. He won't even remember that he used to have four legs. He'll think he's just like all the other dogs."

Lizzie rolled over so she didn't have to look at her mom. "I'm not sure I can handle fostering him," she said into her blanket. "I think maybe this girl Harper should take him instead."

Mom just laughed. "Don't be silly," she said. "You have so much experience taking care of puppies. We'll all help, and it'll be just fine." She put a hand on Lizzie's shoulder. "Now, come on. Get up and come with me. I want to show you something."

Reluctantly, Lizzie followed Mom down to her study, where Dad and Charles sat at the computer. "Check it out, Lizzie!" said Charles. "Watch this guy run!"

Lizzie peered over Dad's shoulder to watch the video of a bunch of dogs racing along a beach. They were so happy and free! Then the camera zoomed in on one of the dogs, a small brown-and-white pup that reminded her of Sparky. Lizzie gasped. That dog, who was darting here and there as he chased the waves, had three legs.

It was one thing to hear people say it, but it was another to see it with her own eyes. The video finished, and another one started. Another bunch of dogs, this time at a dog park. They chased and ran and wrestled. Again, the camera zoomed in, on a smallish Lab mix with a shiny black coat—and three legs. Lizzie couldn't help smiling. The dog's tail whipped back and forth as she played. Her eyes shone with happy mischief as she grabbed a stick and ran with it, zooming around the fenced area with the other dogs chasing her.

"Just like any other dog," Lizzie said out loud.

Dad eased his way out of the office chair and let Lizzie take his place. She clicked on another video, and another. Then she found a website all about tripawds, and started reading. She didn't even notice when the others left the room. And when Dr. Jo called a few hours later, Lizzie was ready. She was ready to bring Sparky home.

CHAPTER NINE

Once again, Lizzie and Harper sat in the back-seat of Ms. Dobbins's car, with Sparky nestled between them on a soft bed of blankets. Dr. Jo and Layla waved as they drove away from the surgeon's office. "We'll see you in a week for a checkup," called Dr. Jo. "Call if you have any questions or concerns."

Lizzie stroked Sparky's delicate little nose. She loved the white stripe that ran between his eyes. He blinked at her and yawned.

Ooh, I sure am sleepy. Actually, maybe I'm asleep. But I think I'm having a wonderful dream about being together with all my favorite people again.

"Do you think he remembers us?" Harper asked.

"No question," said Lizzie.

"Absolutely," agreed Ms. Dobbins. "Did you see the way he was sniffing at my sleeve?" She stopped for a red light and turned back to look at him. "Aww, the cutie. Don't worry, hon—we'll get you settled in at the Petersons' and you can get the rest you need. They'll take good care of you."

Lizzie was glad that Ms. Dobbins and Harper were coming with her as she brought Sparky home. The puppy's sleeping spot was already all set up for him: a crate in Lizzie's room with all the softest blankets they could find. Lizzie was happy that he would be sleeping in her room, where she could keep a close eye on him. They'd set up another bed in the den downstairs, where he could be closer to the daytime family action but still in his own spot, separate from Buddy. He wouldn't be able to run and play until he was healed.

"That's often the problem," Dr. Jo had said. "These dogs are usually eager to get back to their lives, but it's better if we keep them pretty quiet for the first week or so. We'll see how he's doing next week. By then maybe he'll be ready for more activity. He's young and healthy, so I think he'll heal quickly."

Sparky was welcomed by a very hushed greeting committee: Mom, Dad, and Charles met them at the door, speaking in quiet voices and moving carefully. The Bean hung back, behind Mom's knees, staring wide-eyed at the big bandage on Sparky's hip. Lizzie had already explained to her youngest brother that Sparky had a boo-boo and wouldn't be able to play for a while. "He can't even play with Buddy," Lizzie had told the Bean. "We are going to have to keep the puppies separate for a while." Lizzie knew it wasn't going to be easy, but thanks to all the help she'd had, she did feel ready.

"Are you sure it's okay to have him here?" Ms. Dobbins asked Mom. "I wish I could take him, but I'm away at work for such long hours every day, and I don't think he should be at Caring Paws with me so soon after surgery." She reached out longingly to pet Sparky's little head.

Mom nodded, patting Ms. Dobbins's shoulder. "He'll be fine here, and you're welcome to visit whenever you like."

As Dr. Jo had predicted, Sparky slept all that evening. After supper, Lizzie carried him out back and helped steady him while he peed. Then they went up to her room, and he slept soundly through the whole night. When she woke in the morning, she remembered right away that he was there. She sat up in her bed and looked over at Sparky's crate. He was awake, his head up and alert. He stared back at her with his ears perked and his head tilted.

Whew, that was quite a nap. Now what should we do?

The little dog began to struggle to his feet. "Sparky, wait!" Lizzie said. She threw off her blankets and jumped out of bed so she could help him.

From that moment on, it was hard to keep Sparky still. Sure, he took long naps every day, according to the reports Mom gave Lizzie each afternoon when she got home from school. "But he always perks up when Ms. Dobbins comes to visit," she'd add.

Ms. Dobbins was a regular visitor, showing up every day on her lunch hour. She brought a new kind of treat every day, and fluffy toys, and a really fancy new collar—red leather with silver hearts on it. "I think those visits are the high point of his day," Mom said toward the end of the week. "He just loves to cuddle and kiss and sit on someone's lap."

Lizzie couldn't help feeling a little left out, even though she had plenty of time with Sparky in the mornings and evenings. It was never easy to leave their foster puppies at home when she had to go to school, and this time it was harder than ever. One day, Harper came over and spent practically the whole day with Sparky. That wasn't fair!

Every day, Lizzie raced home, eager to see how Sparky was doing. And every day, he was better and better. They still weren't letting him go up and down stairs, but he could walk from the den to the kitchen without any help, and as long as Lizzie carried him down the outside stairs he could pee on his own in the backyard. He and Buddy had gotten to know each other, and while Lizzie still wasn't allowing the two of them to play outdoors, they had enjoyed several naps together on the couch.

On Friday after school, Lizzie burst into the house, already calling for Mom. She'd had a great idea about how they should take Sparky somewhere new, maybe to the playground, so he could start getting used to different places. "Mom!" she yelled as she squatted to pet Buddy in the front hall. "Mom, where are you? And where is Sparky?"

Mom came down the stairs from her office. "Ms. Dobbins took him to Caring Paws," she said.

"What?" Lizzie stared at her. "Like, she's going to let someone adopt him already?" Lizzie wasn't ready for that.

Mom shook her head. "Oh, no, nothing like that. She just thought Sparky was ready for a change of scene, since he's doing so well. She said she made him a nice little nest in a crate by the reception desk, where he can watch people come and go."

Lizzie was quiet for a moment. It was funny that Ms. Dobbins and she had come up with the same idea—but Lizzie was disappointed that Sparky wasn't there to greet her.

"Sparky will be back by dinnertime," Mom said. She must have noticed the way Lizzie's face had fallen. "In the meantime, I'm sure Buddy would love to play with you."

Lizzie nodded, pulling Buddy toward her for a hug. She knew Ms. Dobbins had done the right thing, but still, she missed Sparky. She'd fallen in love with the spunky little pup—and she was starting to get the feeling that somebody else had, too.

That night, Ms. Dobbins brought Sparky back to the Petersons' just before dinner. "He had a great time," she reported, "and everybody loves him." She told them how Sparky, safe inside a cozy kennel by the reception desk, had greeted each visitor to Caring Paws with happy yips and tail wagging. "You're a real people person, aren't you?" she asked the pup in her arms.

Sparky gazed up at her with sparkly, mischievous eyes.

Especially when it comes to you!

Ms. Dobbins helped Lizzie tuck Sparky into his crate. She kissed the top of his head. "I'll see you tomorrow, Mister," she said.

"Should I bring him to Caring Paws when I come to volunteer?" Lizzie asked. Saturday was her regular day.

"Absolutely," said Ms. Dobbins. "I think he gets a lot out of it, and people love seeing him. I think it's fantastic for folks to see how well a three-legged dog can do, even so soon after surgery." She petted Sparky's head one more time. "He's like a poster boy for tripawds."

"Won't you stay for dinner?" Mom asked as Ms. Dobbins was leaving.

Lizzie could see that Ms. Dobbins was tempted—probably because it would mean a little more time with Sparky. But she shook her head. "Thanks, but I've got some phone calls to make and emails to write."

After Ms. Dobbins left, Lizzie helped Mom set the table. "Ms. Dobbins works all the time, doesn't she?" Lizzie said.

Mom nodded. "Running a shelter takes a lot of work."

"Don't you think Ms. Dobbins could use a

friend?" Lizzie said. "A companion?" Lizzie had been thinking about it all afternoon.

Mom stopped putting down forks and looked at Lizzie. "Are you seriously thinking that she might adopt Sparky?" she asked. "I thought she's always said she'll never adopt a dog."

Lizzie raised an eyebrow. "That's what she always said," she agreed. Then she grinned. "Until she met Sparky, that is."

CHAPTER TEN

On Saturday, Lizzie couldn't wait to tell Harper what she'd been thinking, but she didn't have a chance until they had finished sweeping and mopping the kennel area and were taking a break out in the fenced dog run. They'd brought Sparky and Petey out with them, just to give them both a little outdoor time. Petey moseyed around slowly, sniffing each spot very thoroughly before moving on to the next.

Sparky wasn't exactly zooming around yet like the dogs in the videos, but he would have tried to if Lizzie hadn't held tight to his leash. "Sorry, pal," she told him. "I know you're feeling peppy, but you need more time to heal." Sparky made his way around the yard on three legs, hardly even limping. He sniffed and snuffled and peed, just like any other dog would.

Lots of great smells here! I love this place.

"Well, Sparky sure does seem to enjoy being here at Caring Paws," said Harper, smiling down at the happy pup. "Did you see how he was watching everything that was going on out at reception?"

"Exactly!" said Lizzie. "I've been thinking. Remember those cats at Dr. Jo's office—Yogi and Moxie? The ones they called the office mascots? I think Sparky would be the perfect mascot for Caring Paws." She explained why she thought Sparky could be the exception to Ms. Dobbins's rule of never adopting a dog. "I'm just not sure how we can convince Ms. Dobbins to adopt him," she said finally, wondering if Harper would think the idea was ridiculous.

But Harper grinned at her and held up a hand for a high five. "Great idea. And as for how, it's obvious that Ms. Dobbins is already crazy about Sparky. All we really have to do is make sure she falls even more in love." She knelt down to scoop Sparky gently into her arms. "Right, Sparky?" she asked, kissing him on his adorable little nose.

Sparky blinked up at her and tilted his head to one side.

Whatever you say!

Harper and Lizzie giggled. Lizzie smiled at her new friend. Ms. Dobbins had been right—Lizzie was glad that Harper came on Saturdays. She was a lot of help, and she was fun to be around.

"Hey, guess what?" Harper asked Lizzie. "Speaking of adopting, I think I've convinced my parents that we should give Petey a home. He won't be any trouble at all."

"That's fantastic!" said Lizzie.

"I'm going to bring my mom and dad to meet Petey tomorrow," Harper said. "Maybe you can come, too. And that way you'd have an excuse to bring Sparky here again."

"Yes!" said Lizzie. "Ms. Dobbins needs to see him every single day. She'll get so used to having him around that she won't ever want to give him up." Lizzie smiled down at the pup, who had crawled into her lap for a nap. "Just think, Sparky! If things go our way, we'll be seeing you all the time."

Lizzie and Harper did everything they could to bring Ms. Dobbins and Sparky together. At the end of the day on Sunday, Lizzie suggested that Ms. Dobbins should just take him home for the night. "My mom has work to do tomorrow," she said, "so she won't be home to care for him." She gave Harper a secret smile when Ms. Dobbins agreed.

On Monday, Ms. Dobbins brought Sparky back to Caring Paws for the day. When Harper got there to volunteer, she made sure that she was busy with other tasks so that Ms. Dobbins had to take care of Sparky.

Soon, Sparky was basically living with Ms. Dobbins, either at her home or at Caring Paws. On the afternoon of Sparky's appointment for a checkup, Ms. Dobbins and Harper picked Lizzie up after school. Sparky was already in the car, sitting next to Harper in the middle of the backseat, snuggled cozily into a familiar nest of blankets. Lizzie opened the door and climbed in next to him. "Sparky! I've missed you so much." She leaned over to kiss him, and he kissed her back, thumping his tail on the blankets.

Great to see you again, friend!

Lizzie grinned at Harper. "He really is the cutest tripawd ever," she said.

"He is. In fact, he's literally the cutest puppy in the entire universe," Ms. Dobbins said from the driver's seat.

Harper raised her eyebrows as she grinned back at Lizzie. "He's doing really well, too. Isn't he Ms. Dobbins?" Harper said, laughing. "Remember how excited he was yesterday at Caring Paws when you gave him that hamburger squeaky toy?"

Ms. Dobbins laughed, too.

Lizzie bit her lip. That old jealous feeling washed over her, knotting up her stomach in a familiar way. She felt left out since she'd been at school instead of at Caring Paws. But she shook it off. Why waste time feeling jealous of a great new friend like Harper? "How's Petey doing?" she asked instead. She was so glad that Harper's parents had agreed to adopt him.

"I think he's really happy to have a home," said Harper. "And our other two dogs already love him." She told Lizzie about the cozy bed she'd set up for him, and all the good treats he was enjoying.

Soon Ms. Dobbins pulled up at Dr. Jo's. Lizzie walked into the surgeon's office, feeling very different this time from how she'd felt a week ago. Back then, Lizzie had hoped more than anything that Dr. Jo would be able to fix Sparky's leg. Today, she was hoping for something entirely different. She and Harper exchanged a secret wink as they followed Ms. Dobbins, who was carrying Sparky like a baby in her arms, into the exam room.

"Welcome back, Sparky!" said Dr. Jo as Ms.

Dobbins handed him over. "My, don't you look fantastic. Somebody has been taking very good care of you."

"Many somebodies," said Ms. Dobbins. "It's been a group effort."

Dr. Jo did a quick exam, leaving the bandage off this time so that Lizzie could see the stitches running across Sparky's hip. "We'll take those out in a week or so," said Dr. Jo. "But in the meantime, he's free to do a little more each day. We want him to start getting stronger now, and there are all kinds of exercises you can teach him to help with that. I'll give you a handout when you leave."

"That's wonderful news!" said Ms. Dobbins. Lizzie could see that she was near tears.

"And I would say you can definitely start looking for a permanent, loving home for Sparky," said Dr. Jo. "I spoke to Lizzie about it last night"—she gave Lizzie a wink—"and we agreed that Sparky's home will have to be with someone with an open heart, lots of love to give, and, ideally, a workplace where dogs are welcome."

Ms. Dobbins burst out laughing.

"I'm pretty sure I know why you're laughing," said Harper.

"I'm pretty sure I do, too," said Lizzie. "Dr. Jo just described the perfect home for Sparky. And— I have a feeling he's already found it!" She smiled at Ms. Dobbins. "What do you think?" she asked.

Ms. Dobbins nodded. This time, her tears began to flow. "He sure has," she said. "This boy has found his home." She scooped him carefully off the exam table to give him a hug. "You and me, Sparky," she said, holding him close.

Lizzie and Harper gave each other a high five and a hug. Then they each gave the same to Dr. Jo. "We did it," said Harper.

"Actually," said Lizzie. "Sparky did it."

PUPPY TIPS

Have you ever met a tripawd? They are more common than you would think. You might not even notice one at first at the dog park or on the beach, since many of them zoom around just as fast and play just as hard as all the other dogs. Your parents can help you find some videos like the ones Lizzie watched, and you'll be as impressed as I was by the tripawd spirit!

Dear Reader,

I always wanted to write about a three-legged dog, but I wasn't sure how the story should go. Then my friend Jennifer adopted her adorable tripawd puppy, Choṭi Jyotī, and I was so inspired by her stories and pictures. (Her name means "Little Light" in Hindi.) Sparky's story is different from Jyotī's, but they have a lot in common, too. If you're interested, you can check out her page on Instagram, @choti_jyoti.

Yours from the Puppy Place,

Ellen Miles

DON'T MISS THE NEXT PUPPY PLACE ADVENTURE!

Here's a peek at Donut

"Here's Buckley!" Lizzie Peterson led an excited Yorkie into the reception area at Bowser's Backyard, her aunt's doggy daycare center. Buckley pulled at the leash when he saw who was waiting for him.

"Buckley!" The woman knelt down and opened her arms, and Lizzie let the leash drop so the little dog could dash into his owner's embrace. She loved seeing people and their dogs reunited at the end of the day. It was her favorite time to help out at Aunt Amanda's.

"He was a good boy today," Lizzie told Buckley's owner. "I hear he had a lot of fun with Lena and Skye." Lena and Skye were sister puppies, almost but not quite identical. They were both happy, fluffy, bouncy poodle mixes with pretty brown-and-cream coats. Lizzie knew that they both loved to play.

Lizzie waved good-bye to Buckley as she went back to the kennels to fetch another dog whose owner was waiting. It was Friday, which meant that the dogs would be with their people all weekend. Everybody was in a good mood about that.

Lizzie was excited about the weekend, too. Her aunt had invited her to Camp Bowser, her doggy sleepaway camp in the country. They would be driving up tomorrow, and Lizzie couldn't wait. It was always a treat to spend time there with Aunt

Amanda, who was possibly the only person in the world who was more dog-crazy than Lizzie. On top of that, Aunt Amanda knew so much about dogs and was always happy to share her knowledge with Lizzie.

Lizzie had loved dogs for as long as she could remember. She loved playing with them, training them, cuddling with them, and learning about them. Besides helping her aunt, she also volunteered at the local animal shelter, and she even had a dog-walking business. On top of all that, she and her younger brothers, Charles and the Bean, had managed to convince their parents to let them foster puppies. Now the Petersons were a foster family who took care of puppies who needed homes.

Best of all, Lizzie had her own puppy: the best puppy ever, Buddy. He had started out as a foster puppy, but when the whole family had fallen in love, they had decided to keep him forever.

"Can Buddy come to Camp Bowser with us?" she asked her aunt as they got ready to sweep and mop the kennels after all the dogs had left.

"Aw, I love Buddy, you know that," said Aunt Amanda. "But this time it's just going to be us and Bowser, remember? We have a lot to do if we're going to plan that clicker-training workshop."

Lizzie nodded. "Right," she said. "Got it." She was flattered that Aunt Amanda had asked for her help this weekend. They were going to work on a new workshop that her aunt wanted to start offering. Lizzie had heard of clicker training, but she'd never tried it—which, according to Aunt Amanda, was perfect. Lizzie hoped she wouldn't let Aunt Amanda down.

"You and Bowser will be learning at the same time," her aunt had said. "We'll keep a training diary and see how much we can do in one weekend.

ABOUT THE AUTHOR

Ellen Miles loves dogs, which is why she has a great time writing the Puppy Place books. And guess what? She loves cats, too! (In fact, her very first pet was a beautiful tortoiseshell cat named Jenny.) That's why she came up with the Kitty Corner series. Ellen lives in Vermont and loves to be outdoors with her dog, Zipper, every day, walking, biking, skiing, or swimming, depending on the season. She also loves to read, cook, explore her beautiful state, play with dogs, and hang out with friends and family.

Visit Ellen at ellenmiles.net.